To my husband, David,

who knows what all the colors are made of

—E. T.

To kids everywhere—be Blue! Be you!

—J. C.

BEACH LANE BOOKS •
An imprint of Simon & Schuster Children's
Publishing Division • 1230 Avenue of the Americas,
New York, New York 10020 • Text © 2022 by Ellen Tarlow •
Illustration © 2022 by Julien Chung • Book design © 2022 by
Simon & Schuster, Inc. • All rights reserved, including the right of
reproduction in whole or in part in any form. • BEACH LANE BOOKS
and colophon are trademarks of Simon & Schuster, Inc. • For information
about special discounts for bulk purchases, please contact Simon & Schuster
Special Sales at 1-866-506-1949 or business@simonandschuster.com. • The
Simon & Schuster Speakers Bureau can bring authors to your live event. For
more information or to book an event, contact the Simon & Schuster Speakers
Bureau at 1-866-248-3049 or visit our website at www.simonspeakers.com. •
The text for this book was set in Ionic No 5. • The illustrations for this book
were rendered digitally. • Manufactured in China • 0422 SCP • First Edition •
10 9 8 7 6 5 4 3 2 1 • Library of Congress Cataloging-in-Publication Data •
Names: Tarlow, Ellen, author. | Chung, Julien, illustrator. • Title: Becoming Blue /
Ellen Tarlow ; illustrated by Julien Chung. • Description: First edition. | New
York : Beach Lane Books, 2022. | Audience: Ages 0–8. | Audience: Grades K-1. |
Summary: Blue thinks being Red must be exciting since Red gets to fight
fires and tell cars to stop, but when Blue tries being Red for the day he
realizes the best thing to be is yourself. • Identifiers: LCCN 2021039800
(print) | LCCN 2021039801 (ebook) | ISBN 9781665900010 (hardcover) |
ISBN 9781665900027 (ebook) • Subjects: CYAC: Color—Fiction. |
Individuality—Fiction. | Self-realization—Fiction. | LCGFT:
Picture books. • Classification: LCC PZ7.T174 Be 2022 (print) |
LCC PZ7.T174 (ebook) | DDC [E]—dc23 • LC record
available at https://lccn.loc.gov/2021039800 •
LC ebook record available at https://
lccn.loc.gov/2021039801

BECOMING BLUE

written by
Ellen Tarlow

illustrated by
Julien Chung

Beach Lane Books

New York London Toronto Sydney New Delhi

Blue wanted to be Red.
Red was always up to something.
And it was always fascinating.

She might be dangling from a tree,
dancing with her friends.

(Blue wondered how they knew all the right moves.)

Or she was rushing to put out a fire.

"Wait for me!" cried Blue.

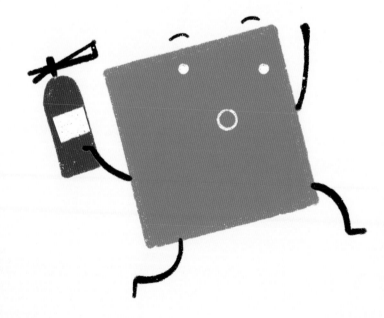

Sometimes, Red *was* the fire.
(Blue was a little scared to try that one.)

And just when you thought Red
couldn't BE any more exciting,
she would pop up in the middle of
traffic saying her best word:

Everyone stopped.

(This wasn't as easy as it looked.)

"Please consider stopping," said Blue
as the cars whizzed right past.

When Red arrived, everyone paid attention. She knew the funniest jokes.

(Or maybe it was the way she told them.)

When Red was sad, no one seemed sadder.

And when she was mad . . .

well, Blue didn't stick around
long enough to find out.

Then one day, Blue was making
valentines when Red turned to him
and out came her best word again.

Blue dropped his scissors.
"Who?" he asked. "Me?"

YES!

yelled Red. "You!
Stop copying me!
You are Blue.
Go be Blue!"

Blue turned as Red as Blue could
(which wasn't very Red).

And then he went away.

What did Red mean, Be Blue?
What *was* Blue?

He tried to think Blue thoughts.
He tried to feel Blue feelings.
And before he knew it, he was crying.
Blue cried and cried.

And then something happened.
Blue felt soft. He felt flowy.

He was a river!
"Oooh," said Blue.
He flowed, and he gurgled, and then
he looked up at the sky.
Wow! It was Blue up there, too!
How had he never noticed?

Soon Blue was enjoying being
Blue all the time.
There were birds and flowers
and clear thoughts.

There were lakes and oceans
and also sad songs
that somehow made you feel happy.

Once he met Red at a fire.

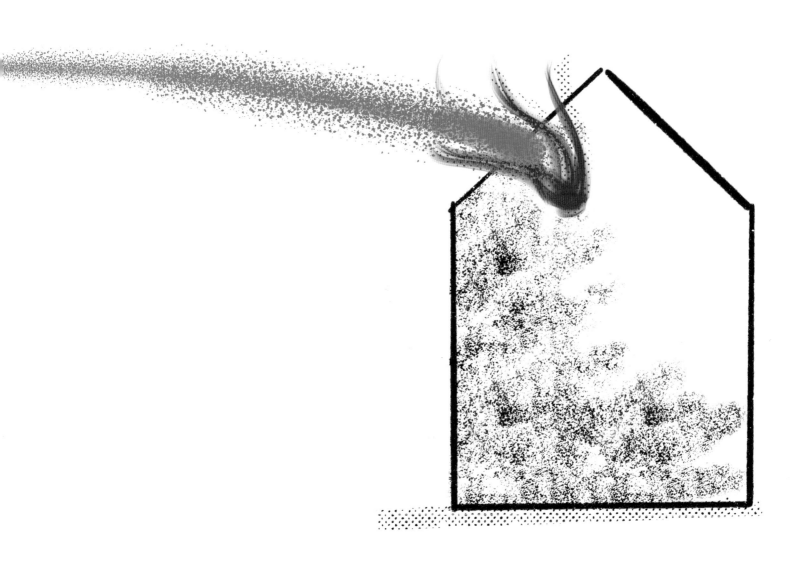

"Good work!" called Blue after the fire was out.
"Thanks to you!" said Red.
She looked impressed.

Now when Blue wasn't busy being Blue,
he and Red would play.
Sometimes he would be Red.
(It was easier now.)

And Red would try Blue things.

"Tell me how you flow again," she said.

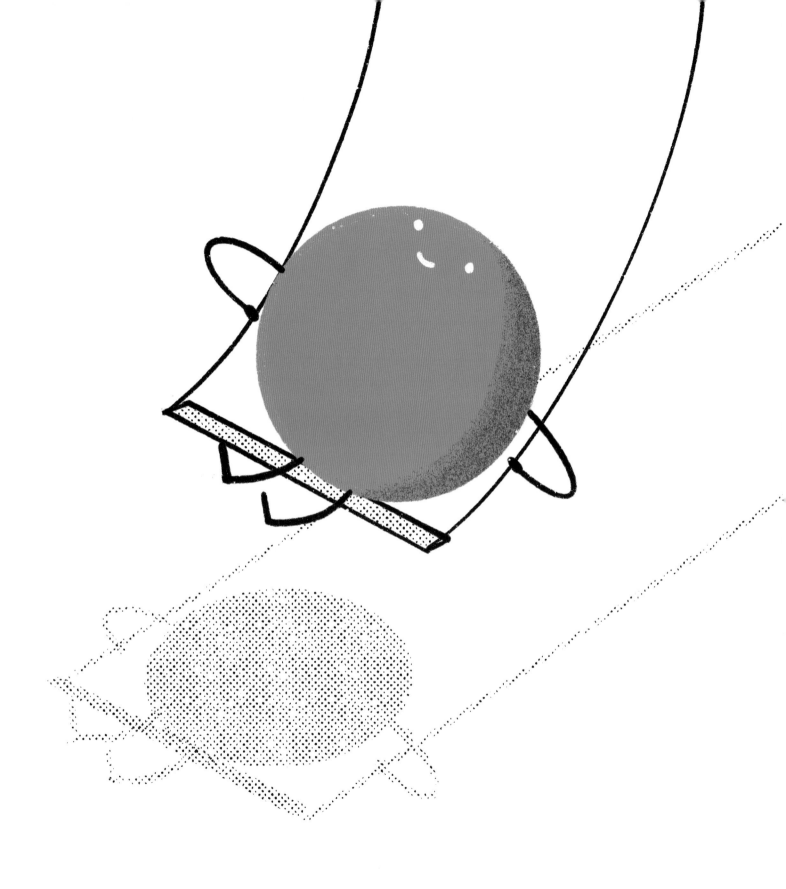

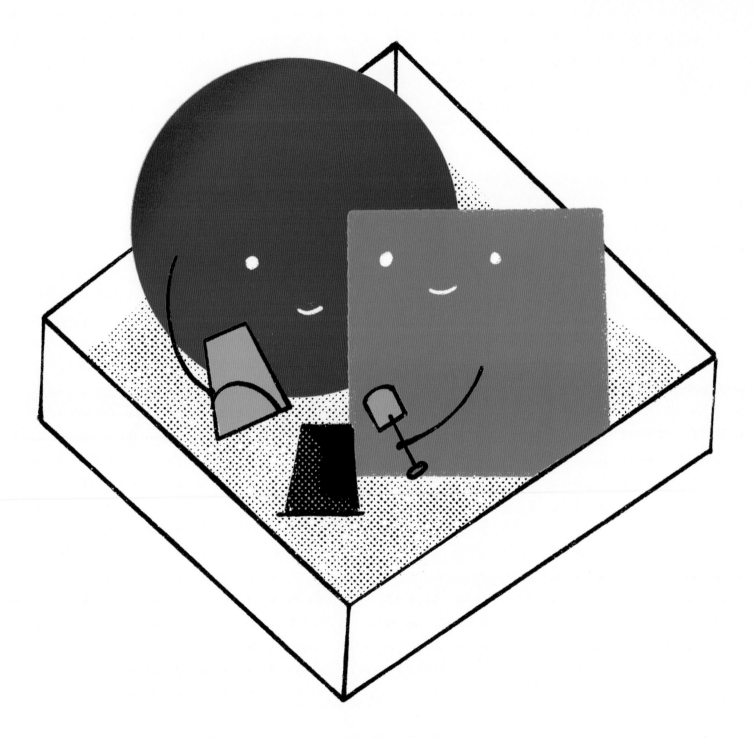

And one day, they discovered
the most fun thing yet.
It was called . . .

being Purple!